For Shira who always believed in me

thank you

Benguin the penguin was lounging around on top of his iceberg thinking about his tummy

Temimah the walrus slid by with a nice juicy fish in her mouth. Benguin saw the fish and so did his tummy. Benguin the penguin decided to get a fish for HIS tummy.
So off he went down the iceberg.

As he was walking he hummed a fish tummy tune to himself and bumped into his friend Puffy the Puffin. "Where are you going?" asked Puffy worriedly.

"I am going to get a fish for my tummy" Benguin stated with pride. He was proud because he had thought of the idea himself.

"What if there are no fish left?" worried Puffy.
Benguin hadn't thought of this before. Puffin
flew away and left Benguin with his worries.

He slowly continued down the hill worrying about
the fish and if his tummy would ever be full.
He was so busy thinking about his lost fish that
he didn't even notice a black tail buried in the
snow.

Hermione the Ermine was weaseling around in the snow and Benguin stepped on her tail causing her to swallow a mouthful of snow in shock!

Angrily she yelled at him, "What are you doing waddling around here thinking only of yourself!"

Benguin, getting over the shock of being yelled at by Hermione, forgot his worries and now he felt angry.

"I am going to get a fish for MY tummy!" He yelled waddle-stomping away.

Hermione yelled after him, "I hope someone steps on your tail!"

Benguin was waddle-stomping down the hill with Hermione's anger. "No one will step on MY tail when I get my fish!" He muttered furiously to his tummy.

Rocky the Ptarmigan was sitting stoically in the middle of the path on her egg. "Move!" Bellowed Benguin to Rocky.
"What for?" Rocky asked glumly.
"I am hungry and am getting a fish for my tummy.

Rocky sighed her sad sigh. "Why bother? What is the point? After you get your fish and eat it you will just be hungry again."

Benguin hung his head as he went around Rocky. "Why bother?" he asked his tummy forlornly. Rocky had a point, he would just be hungry again.

When he finally arrived at the ice's edge he slumped down in sorrow, too sad to even look for his tummy's fish.

Bina the whale swam up to the surface for some air. As she swam along she stuck her eye out of the water scanning the horizon and spotted the most miserable penguin she had ever seen.

Being the large creature that she was, she could hold more than one feeling at a time. She liked to help the smaller creatures whose problems felt smaller to her.

Picking up a few fish, she made her way to the forlorn creature. "What is wrong?" She asked. "There are no fish." He answered.

Bina lovingly laid the fish she had collected at his feet. "But, but, Puffy said, there are no fish left, " he wailed.
"Well that is not true, as I have brought you some right now and there are more where those came from."

"But, but," worried Benguin, "Hermione said someone will step on my tail and I will lose those fish."

Bina looked at him. "Turn around." She said. Benguin turned slowly around. She looked at his tail. "I don't see anything on your tail except your feather," she commented.

"But, but," stuttered Benguin, "Rocky said that after I eat this fish I will just get hungry again!"

"Then what will you do?" Asked Bina curiously.

"Well...." He hadn't thought of that!

"I guess I could just get another fish"
"So, why are you sad again?" She asked smiling at him.
"I'm not!" Benguin realized!

Benguin ate his fish and with his full tummy began to go back up the hill.

Waddling contentedly along with his delightfully full tummy Benguin came up to Rocky sitting dejectedly on her egg.

"Oh, you again, I guess you had your fish already?"'

"Yes', he said patting his full tummy, "I had lots of fish and they were delicious!"

Rocky looked down sadly at her egg, "You will probably get a tummy ache then", she frowned "I always do after fish."

Benguin felt his tummy, it seemed ok to him. He never had a tummy ache from fish before, and chances are he wouldn't have one now. "I don't have your bird tummy", he responded. "My tummy feels okay", and he continued up the slope.

Hermione was storming down the hill huffing and puffing. She took one look at Benguin and shouted, "I hope your tail hurts from everyone stepping on it!!"

Benguin looked her squarely in the eye. "No one stepped on my tail at all. I am sorry for stepping on yours though."

"Well, well...watch where you are going in the future!" She hollered and stomped off.

Benguin watched her go. He clicked his beak and carried on up the hill.

Puffy was flying by and spotted Benguin ambling his way up the icy slope. Landing on his head when he reached the top, Puffy anxiously inquired how the fish meal was coming along.

Benguin happily stuck out his delightfully full tummy to show the bird.

"What if there are no fish tomorrow when you are hungry again?" Puffy asked.

Benguin shifted his feet (Puffy was heavier than he looked) and thought about it. "There are plenty of fish in the sea." He answered happily.

Made in the USA
Middletown, DE
08 October 2023

39794884R00015